AN HONEST THIEF

BY

FYODOR DOSTOEVSKY

First Published in 1848

British Library Cataloguing-in-Publication Data
A catalogue record for this book is available
from the British Library

CONTENTS

Fyodor Dostoevsky

Fyodor Mikhailovich Dostoevsky was born in Moscow, as the second son of a former army doctor. Raised within the grounds of the Mariinsky hospital, at an early age he was introduced to English, French, German and Russian literature, as well as to fairy-tales and legends. He was educated at home and at a private school, but shortly after the death of his mother in 1837, he was sent to St. Petersburg, where he entered the Army Engineering College.

In 1839 Dostoevsky's father died. A year later, Dostoevsky graduated as a military engineer, but resigned in 1844 to devote himself to writing. While earning money from translations, he wrote his first novel, *Poor Folk,* which appeared in 1846. It was followed by *The Double* (1846), which depicted a man who was haunted by a look-alike who eventually usurps his position.

In 1846, Dostoevsky joined a group of utopian socialists. He was arrested in 1849 and sentenced to death. After a mock execution, his sentence was reduced to imprisonment in Siberia. Dostoevsky spent four years in hard labour – ten years later, he would turn these experiences into *The House of the Dead* (1860). Upon his release, he joined the army in Semipalatinsk (North-East Kazakhstan), where he remained for a further four years.

Dostoevsky returned to St. Petersburg in 1854. Three years later, he married Maria Isaev, a 29-year old widow. He resigned from the army in 1859, and focussed once more on writing. Between the years 1861 and 1863 he served as editor of the monthly periodical *Time*, which was later suppressed because of an article on the Polish uprising.

In 1864-65 his wife and brother died and Dostoevsky was burdened with debts. The situation was made worse by his own lifelong gambling addiction. From the turmoil of the 1860s emerged his classic *Notes from the Underground* (1864), a psychological study of a social outcast seeking spiritual rebirth. The novel marked a watershed in Dostoevsky's artistic development.

Notes from the Underground (1864) was followed by Dostoevsky's most famous work, *Crime and Punishment* (1866). An account of an individual's fall and redemption, and an implicit critique of nihilism, it is now regarded as one of the greatest works of Russian literature. Two years later *The Idiot* (1868) was published, and three years after that came *The Possessed*, (1871) an exploration of philosophical nihilism.

In 1867 Dostoevsky married Anna Snitkin, his 22-year old stenographer. They travelled abroad and returned in 1871. By the time the *The Brothers Karamazov* was published, between 1879-80, Dostoevsky was recognized in his own country as one of its great writers. However, having suffered from a fragile mental disposition his whole life, Dostoevsky began to succumb to larger periods of mania and rage. After a particularly bad epileptic fit, he died in St. Petersburg in early 1881, aged 59.

Together with Leo Tolstoy, Dostoevsky is now regarded as one of the greatest and most influential novelists in all of Russian literature. His books have been translated into more than 170 languages and have sold around 15 million copies.

AN HONEST THIEF

One morning, just as I was about to set off to my office, Agrafena, my cook, washerwoman and housekeeper, came in to me and, to my surprise, entered into conversation.

She had always been such a silent, simple creature that, except her daily inquiry about dinner, she had not uttered a word for the last six years. I, at least, had heard nothing else from her.

"Here I have come in to have a word with you, sir," she began abruptly; "you really ought to let the little room."

"Which little room?"

"Why, the one next the kitchen, to be sure."

"What for?"

"What for? Why because folks do take in lodgers, to be sure."

"But who would take it?"

"Who would take it? Why, a lodger would take it, to be sure."

"But, my good woman, one could not put a bedstead in it; there wouldn't be room to move! Who could live in it?"

"Who wants to live there! As long as he has a place to sleep in. Why, he would live in the window."

"In what window?"

"In what window! As though you didn't know! The one in the passage, to be sure. He would sit there, sewing or doing anything else. Maybe he would sit on a chair, too. He's got a chair; and he has a table, too; he's got everything."

7

"Who is 'he' then?"

"Oh, a good man, a man of experience. I will cook for him. And I'll ask him three roubles a month for his board and lodging."

After prolonged efforts I succeeded at last in learning from Agrafena that an elderly man had somehow managed to persuade her to admit him into the kitchen as a lodger and boarder. Any notion Agrafena took into her head had to be carried out; if not, I knew she would give me no peace. When anything was not to her liking, she at once began to brood, and sank into a deep dejection that would last for a fortnight or three weeks. During that period my dinners were spoiled, my linen was mislaid, my floors went unscrubbed; in short, I had a great deal to put up with. I had observed long ago that this inarticulate woman was incapable of conceiving a project, of originating an idea of her own. But if anything like a notion or a project was by some means put into her feeble brain, to prevent its being carried out meant, for a time, her moral assassination. And so, as I cared more for my peace of mind than for anything else, I consented forthwith.

"Has he a passport anyway, or something of the sort?"

"To be sure, he has. He is a good man, a man of experience; three roubles he's promised to pay."

The very next day the new lodger made his appearance in my modest bachelor quarters; but I was not put out by this, indeed I was inwardly pleased. I lead as a rule a very lonely hermit's existence. I have scarcely any friends; I hardly ever go anywhere. As I had spent ten years never coming out of my shell, I had, of course, grown used to solitude. But another ten or fifteen years or more of the same solitary existence, with the same Agrafena, in the same bachelor quarters, was in truth a somewhat cheerless prospect. And therefore a new inmate, if well-behaved, was a heaven-sent blessing.

Agrafena had spoken truly: my lodger was certainly a man of experience. From his passport it appeared that he was an old soldier, a fact which I should have known indeed from his face. An old soldier is easily recognised. Astafy Ivanovitch was a favourable specimen of his class. We got on very well together. What was best of all, Astafy Ivanovitch would sometimes tell a story, describing some incident in his own life. In the perpetual boredom of my existence such a story-teller was a veritable treasure. One day he told me one of these stories. It made an impression on me. The following event was what led to it.

I was left alone in the flat; both Astafy and Agrafena were out on business of their own. All of a sudden I heard from the inner room somebody—I fancied a stranger—come in; I went out; there actually was a stranger in the passage, a short fellow wearing no overcoat in spite of the cold autumn weather.

"What do you want?"

"Does a clerk called Alexandrov live here?"

"Nobody of that name here, brother. Good-bye."

"Why, the dvornik told me it was here," said my visitor, cautiously retiring towards the door.

"Be off, be off, brother, get along."

Next day after dinner, while Astafy Ivanovitch was fitting on a coat which he was altering for me, again some one came into the passage. I half opened the door.

Before my very eyes my yesterday's visitor, with perfect composure, took my wadded greatcoat from the peg and, stuffing it under his arm, darted out of the flat. Agrafena stood all the time staring at him, agape with astonishment and doing nothing for the protection of my property. Astafy Ivanovitch flew in pursuit of the thief and ten minutes later came back out of breath and empty-handed. He had vanished completely.

"Well, there's a piece of luck, Astafy Ivanovitch!"

"It's a good job your cloak is left! Or he would have put you in a plight, the thief!"

But the whole incident had so impressed Astafy Ivanovitch that I forgot the theft as I looked at him. He could not get over it. Every minute or two he would drop the work upon which he was engaged, and would describe over again how it had all happened, how he had been standing, how the greatcoat had been taken down before his very eyes, not a yard away, and how it had come to pass that he could not catch the thief. Then he would sit down to his work again, then leave it once more, and at last I saw him go down to the dvornik to tell him all about it, and to upbraid him for letting such a thing happen in his domain. Then he came back and began scolding Agrafena. Then he sat down to his work again, and long afterwards he was still muttering to himself how it had all happened, how he stood there and I was here, how before our eyes, not a yard away, the thief took the coat off the peg, and so on. In short, though Astafy Ivanovitch understood his business, he was a terrible slow-coach and busy-body.

"He's made fools of us, Astafy Ivanovitch," I said to him in the evening, as I gave him a glass of tea. I wanted to while away the time by recalling the story of the lost greatcoat, the frequent repetition of which, together with the great earnestness of the speaker, was beginning to become very amusing.

"Fools, indeed, sir! Even though it is no business of mine, I am put out. It makes me angry though it is not my coat that was lost. To my thinking there is no vermin in the world worse than a thief. Another takes what you can spare, but a thief steals the work of your hands, the sweat of your brow, your time . . . Ugh, it's nasty! One can't speak of it! it's too vexing. How is it you don't feel the loss of your property, sir?"

"Yes, you are right, Astafy Ivanovitch, better if the thing had been burnt; it's annoying to let the thief have it, it's disagreeable."

"Disagreeable! I should think so! Yet, to be sure, there are thieves and thieves. And I have happened, sir, to come across an honest thief."

"An honest thief? But how can a thief be honest, Astafy Ivanovitch?"

"There you are right indeed, sir. How can a thief be honest? There are none such. I only meant to say that he was an honest man, sure enough, and yet he stole. I was simply sorry for him."

"Why, how was that, Astafy Ivanovitch?"

"It was about two years ago, sir. I had been nearly a year out of a place, and just before I lost my place I made the acquaintance of a poor lost creature. We got acquainted in a public-house. He was a drunkard, a vagrant, a beggar, he had been in a situation of some sort, but from his drinking habits he had lost his work. Such a ne'er-do-weel! God only knows what he had on! Often you wouldn't be sure if he'd a shirt under his coat; everything he could lay his hands upon he would drink away. But he was not one to quarrel; he was a quiet fellow. A soft, good-natured chap. And he'd never ask, he was ashamed; but you could see for yourself the poor fellow wanted a drink, and you would stand it him. And so we got friendly, that's to say, he stuck to me. . . . It was all one to me. And what a man he was, to be sure! Like a little dog he would follow me; wherever I went there he would be; and all that after our first meeting, and he as thin as a thread-paper! At first it was 'let me stay the night'; well, I let him stay.

"I looked at his passport, too; the man was all right.

"Well, the next day it was the same story, and then the third day he came again and sat all day in the window and stayed the night. Well, thinks I, he is sticking to me; give him food and drink and shelter at night, too—here am I, a poor man, and a hanger-on to keep as well! And before he came to me, he used to go in the same way to a government clerk's; he attached himself to him; they were always drinking together; but he, through trouble of some sort, drank himself into the grave. My man was called Emelyan Ilyitch. I pondered and pondered what I was to do with him. To drive him away I was ashamed. I was sorry for him; such a pitiful, God-forsaken creature I never did set eyes on. And not a word said either; he does not ask, but just sits there and looks into your eyes like a dog. To think what drinking will bring a man down to!

"I keep asking myself how am I to say to him: 'You must be moving, Emelyanoushka, there's nothing for you here, you've come to the wrong place; I shall soon not have a bite for myself, how am I to keep you too?'

"I sat and wondered what he'd do when I said that to him. And

I seemed to see how he'd stare at me, if he were to hear me say that, how long he would sit and not understand a word of it. And when it did get home to him at last, how he would get up from the window, would take up his bundle—I can see it now, the red-check handkerchief full of holes, with God knows what wrapped up in it, which he had always with him, and then how he would set his shabby old coat to rights, so that it would look decent and keep him warm, so that no holes would be seen—he was a man of delicate feelings! And how he'd open the door and go out with tears in his eyes. Well, there's no letting a man go to ruin like that. . . . One's sorry for him.

"And then again, I think, how am I off myself? Wait a bit, Emelyanoushka, says I to myself, you've not long to feast with me: I shall soon be going away and then you will not find me.

"Well, sir, our family made a move; and Alexandr Filimonovitch, my master (now deceased, God rest his soul), said, 'I am thoroughly satisfied with you, Astafy Ivanovitch; when we come back from the country we will take you on again.' I had been butler with them; a nice gentleman he was, but he died that same year. Well, after seeing him off, I took my belongings, what little money I had, and I thought I'd have a rest for a time, so I went to an old woman I knew, and I took a corner in her room. There was only one corner free in it. She had been a nurse, so now she had a pension and a room of her own. Well, now good-bye, Emelyanoushka, thinks I, you won't find me now, my boy.

"And what do you think, sir? I had gone out to see a man I knew, and when I came back in the evening, the first thing I saw was Emelyanoushka! There he was, sitting on my box and his check bundle beside him; he was sitting in his ragged old coat, waiting for me. And to while away the time he had borrowed a church book from the old lady, and was holding it wrong side upwards. He'd scented me out! My heart sank. Well, thinks I, there's no help for it—why didn't I turn him out at first? So I asked him straight off: Have you brought your passport, Emelyanoushka?'

"I sat down on the spot, sir, and began to ponder: will a

vagabond like that be very much trouble to me? And on thinking it over it seemed he would not be much trouble. He must be fed, I thought. Well, a bit of bread in the morning, and to make it go down better I'll buy him an onion. At midday I should have to give him another bit of bread and an onion; and in the evening, onion again with kvass, with some more bread if he wanted it. And if some cabbage soup were to come our way, then we should both have had our fill. I am no great eater myself, and a drinking man, as we all know, never eats; all he wants is herb-brandy or green vodka. He'll ruin me with his drinking, I thought, but then another idea came into my head, sir, and took great hold on me. So much so that if Emelyanoushka had gone away I should have felt that I had nothing to live for, I do believe. . . . I determined on the spot to be a father and guardian to him. I'll keep him from ruin, I thought, I'll wean him from the glass! You wait a bit, thought I; very well, Emelyanoushka, you may stay, only you must behave yourself; you must obey orders.

"Well, thinks I to myself, I'll begin by training him to work of some sort, but not all at once; let him enjoy himself a little first, and I'll look round and find something you are fit for, Emelyanoushka. For every sort of work a man needs a special ability, you know, sir. And I began to watch him on the quiet; I soon saw Emelyanoushka was a desperate character. I began, sir, with a word of advice: I said this and that to him. 'Emelyanoushka,' said I, 'you ought to take a thought and mend your ways. Have done with drinking! Just look what rags you go about in: that old coat of yours, if I may make bold to say so, is fit for nothing but a sieve. A pretty state of things! It's time to draw the line, sure enough.' Emelyanoushka sat and listened to me with his head hanging down. Would you believe it, sir? It had come to such a pass with him, he'd lost his tongue through drink and could not speak a word of sense. Talk to him of cucumbers and he'd answer back about beans! He would listen and listen to me and then heave such a sigh. 'What are you sighing for, Emelyan Ilyitch?' I asked him.

"'Oh, nothing; don't you mind me, Astafy Ivanovitch. Do you know there were two women fighting in the street today, Astafy Ivanovitch? One upset the other woman's basket of cranberries by accident.'

"'Well, what of that?'

"'And the second one upset the other's cranberries on purpose and trampled them under foot, too.'

"'Well, and what of it, Emelyan Ilyitch?'

"'Why, nothing, Astafy Ivanovitch, I just mentioned it.'

"'"Nothing, I just mentioned it!" Emelyanoushka, my boy, I thought, you've squandered and drunk away your brains!'

"'And do you know, a gentleman dropped a money-note on the pavement in Gorohovy Street, no, it was Sadovy Street. And a peasant saw it and said, "That's my luck"; and at the same time another man saw it and said, "No, it's my bit of luck. I saw it before you did."'

"'Well, Emelyan Ilyitch?'

"'And the fellows had a fight over it, Astafy Ivanovitch. But a policeman came up, took away the note, gave it back to the gentleman and threatened to take up both the men.'

"'Well, but what of that? What is there edifying about it, Emelyanoushka?'

"'Why, nothing, to be sure. Folks laughed, Astafy Ivanovitch.'

"'Ach, Emelyanoushka! What do the folks matter? You've sold your soul for a brass farthing! But do you know what I have to tell you, Emelyan Ilyitch?'

"'What, Astafy Ivanovitch?'

"'Take a job of some sort, that's what you must do. For the hundredth time I say to you, set to work, have some mercy on yourself!'

"'What could I set to, Astafy Ivanovitch? I don't know what job I could set to, and there is no one who will take me on, Astafy Ivanovitch.'

"'That's how you came to be turned off, Emelyanoushka, you drinking man!'

"'And do you know Vlass, the waiter, was sent for to the office today, Astafy Ivanovitch?'

"'Why did they send for him, Emelyanoushka?' I asked.

"'I could not say why, Astafy Ivanovitch. I suppose they wanted him there, and that's why they sent for him.'

"A-ach, thought I, we are in a bad way, poor Emelyanoushka! The Lord is chastising us for our sins. Well, sir, what is one to do with such a man?

"But a cunning fellow he was, and no mistake. He'd listen and listen to me, but at last I suppose he got sick of it. As soon as he sees I am beginning to get angry, he'd pick up his old coat and out he'd slip and leave no trace. He'd wander about all day and come back at night drunk. Where he got the money from, the Lord only knows; I had no hand in that.

"'No,' said I, 'Emelyan Ilyitch, you'll come to a bad end. Give over drinking, mind what I say now, give it up! Next time you come home in liquor, you can spend the night on the stairs. I won't let you in!'

"After hearing that threat, Emelyanoushka sat at home that day and the next; but on the third he slipped off again. I waited and waited; he didn't come back. Well, at least I don't mind owning, I was in a fright, and I felt for the man too. What have I done to him? I thought. I've scared him away. Where's the poor fellow gone to now? He'll get lost maybe. Lord have mercy upon us!

"Night came on, he did not come. In the morning I went out into the porch; I looked, and if he hadn't gone to sleep in the porch! There he was with his head on the step, and chilled to the marrow of his bones.

"'What next, Emelyanoushka, God have mercy on you! Where will you get to next!'

"'Why, you were—sort of—angry with me, Astafy Ivanovitch, the other day, you were vexed and promised to put me to sleep in the porch, so I didn't—sort of—venture to come in, Astafy Ivanovitch, and so I lay down here. . . .'

"I did feel angry and sorry too.

"'Surely you might undertake some other duty, Emelyanoushka, instead of lying here guarding the steps,' I said.

"'Why, what other duty, Astafy Ivanovitch?'

"'You lost soul'—I was in such a rage, I called him that—'if you could but learn tailoring work! Look at your old rag of a coat! It's not enough to have it in tatters, here you are sweeping the steps with it! You might take a needle and boggle up your rags, as decency demands. Ah, you drunken man!'

"What do you think, sir? He actually did take a needle. Of course I said it in jest, but he was so scared he set to work. He took off his coat and began threading the needle. I watched him; as you may well guess, his eyes were all red and bleary, and his hands were all of a shake. He kept shoving and shoving the thread and could not get it through the eye of the needle; he kept screwing his eyes up and wetting the thread and twisting it in his fingers—it was no good! He gave it up and looked at me.

"'Well,' said I, 'this is a nice way to treat me! If there had been folks by to see, I don't know what I should have done! Why, you simple fellow, I said it you in joke, as a reproach. Give over your nonsense, God bless you! Sit quiet and don't put me to shame, don't sleep on my stairs and make a laughing-stock of me.'

"'Why, what am I to do, Astafy Ivanovitch? I know very well I am a drunkard and good for nothing! I can do nothing but vex you, my bene—bene—factor. . . .'

"And at that his blue lips began all of a sudden to quiver, and a tear ran down his white cheek and trembled on his stubbly chin, and then poor Emelyanoushka burst into a regular flood of tears. Mercy on us! I felt as though a knife were thrust into my heart! The sensitive creature! I'd never have expected it. Who could have guessed it? No, Emelyanoushka, thought I, I shall give you up altogether. You can go your way like the rubbish you are.

"Well, sir, why make a long story of it? And the whole affair is so trifling; it's not worth wasting words upon. Why, you, for instance, sir, would not have given a thought to it, but I would have given a great deal—if I had a great deal to give—that it never should have happened at all.

"I had a pair of riding breeches by me, sir, deuce take them, fine, first-rate riding breeches they were too, blue with a check on it. They'd been ordered by a gentleman from the country, but he would not have them after all; said they were not full enough, so they were left on my hands. It struck me they were worth something. At the second-hand dealer's I ought to get five silver roubles for them, or if not I could turn them into two pairs of trousers for Petersburg gentlemen and have a piece over for a waistcoat for myself. Of course for poor people like us everything comes in. And it happened just then that Emelyanoushka was having a sad time of it. There he sat day after day: he did not drink, not a drop passed his lips, but he sat and moped like an owl. It was sad to see him—he just sat and brooded. Well, thought I, either you've not got a copper to spend, my lad, or else you're turning over a new leaf of yourself, you've given it up, you've listened to reason. Well, sir, that's how it was with us; and just then came a holiday. I went to vespers; when I came home I found Emelyanoushka sitting in the window, drunk and rocking to and fro.

"Ah! so that's what you've been up to, my lad! And I went to get something out of my chest. And when I looked in, the breeches were not there. . . . I rummaged here and there; they'd vanished. When I'd ransacked everywhere and saw they were not there, something seemed to stab me to the heart. I ran first to the old dame and began accusing her; of Emelyanoushka I'd not the faintest suspicion, though there was cause for it in his sitting there drunk.

"'No,' said the old body, 'God be with you, my fine gentleman, what good are riding breeches to me? Am I going to wear such things? Why, a skirt I had I lost the other day through a fellow of your sort . . . I know nothing; I can tell you nothing about it,' she said.

"'Who has been here, who has been in?' I asked.

"'Why, nobody has been, my good sir,' says she; 'I've been here all the while; Emelyan Ilyitch went out and came back again; there he sits, ask him.'

"'Emelyanoushka,' said I, 'have you taken those new riding breeches for anything; you remember the pair I made for that gentleman from the country?'

"'No, Astafy Ivanovitch,' said he; 'I've not—sort of—touched them.'

"I was in a state! I hunted high and low for them—they were nowhere to be found. And Emelyanoushka sits there rocking himself to and fro. I was squatting on my heels facing him and bending over the chest, and all at once I stole a glance at him. . . . Alack, I thought; my heart suddenly grew hot within me and I felt myself flushing up too. And suddenly Emelyanoushka looked at me.

"'No, Astafy Ivanovitch,' said he, 'those riding breeches of yours, maybe, you are thinking, maybe, I took them, but I never touched them.'

"'But what can have become of them, Emelyan Ilyitch?'

"'No, Astafy Ivanovitch,' said he, 'I've never seen them.'

"'Why, Emelyan Ilyitch, I suppose they've run off of themselves, eh?'

"'Maybe they have, Astafy Ivanovitch.'

"When I heard him say that, I got up at once, went up to him, lighted the lamp and sat down to work to my sewing. I was altering a waistcoat for a clerk who lived below us. And wasn't there a burning pain and ache in my breast! I shouldn't have minded so much if I had put all the clothes I had in the fire. Emelyanoushka seemed to have an inkling of what a rage I was in. When a man is guilty, you know, sir, he scents trouble far off, like the birds of the air before a storm.

"'Do you know what, Astafy Ivanovitch,' Emelyanoushka began, and his poor old voice was shaking as he said the words, 'Antip Prohoritch, the apothecary, married the coachman's wife this morning, who died the other day——'

"I did give him a look, sir, a nasty look it was; Emelyanoushka understood it too. I saw him get up, go to the bed, and begin to rummage there for something. I waited—he was busy there a long time and kept muttering all the while, 'No, not there, where can the blessed things have got to!' I waited to see what he'd do; I saw him creep under the bed on all fours. I couldn't bear it any longer. 'What are you crawling about under the bed for, Emelyan Ilyitch?' said I.

"'Looking for the breeches, Astafy Ivanovitch. Maybe they've dropped down there somewhere.'

"'Why should you try to help a poor simple man like me,' said I, 'crawling on your knees for nothing, sir?'—I called him that in my vexation.

"'Oh, never mind, Astafy Ivanovitch, I'll just look. They'll turn up, maybe, somewhere.'

"'H'm,' said I, 'look here, Emelyan Ilyitch!'

"'What is it, Astafy Ivanovitch?' said he.

"'Haven't you simply stolen them from me like a thief and a robber, in return for the bread and salt you've eaten here?' said I.

"I felt so angry, sir, at seeing him fooling about on his knees before me.

"'No, Astafy Ivanovitch.'

"And he stayed lying as he was on his face under the bed. A long time he lay there and then at last crept out. I looked at him and the man was as white as a sheet. He stood up, and sat down near me in the window and sat so for some ten minutes.

"'No, Astafy Ivanovitch,' he said, and all at once he stood up and came towards me, and I can see him now; he looked dreadful. 'No, Astafy Ivanovitch,' said he, 'I never—sort of—touched your breeches.'

"He was all of a shake, poking himself in the chest with a trembling finger, and his poor old voice shook so that I was frightened, sir, and sat as though I was rooted to the window-seat.

"'Well, Emelyan Ilyitch,' said I, 'as you will, forgive me if I, in my foolishness, have accused you unjustly. As for the breeches, let them go hang; we can live without them. We've still our hands, thank God; we need not go thieving or begging from some other poor man; we'll earn our bread.'

"Emelyanoushka heard me out and went on standing there before me. I looked up, and he had sat down. And there he sat all the evening without stirring. At last I lay down to sleep. Emelyanoushka went on sitting in the same place. When I looked out in the morning, he was lying curled up in his old coat on the bare floor; he felt too crushed even to come to bed. Well, sir, I felt no more liking for the fellow from that day, in fact for the first few days I hated him. I felt as one may say as though my own son had robbed me, and done me a deadly hurt. Ach, thought I, Emelyanoushka, Emelyanoushka! And Emelyanoushka, sir, went on drinking for a whole fortnight without stopping. He was drunk all the time, and regularly besotted. He went out in the morning and came back late at night, and for a whole fortnight I didn't get a word out of him. It was as though grief was gnawing at his heart, or as though he wanted to do for himself completely. At last he stopped; he must have come to the end of all he'd got, and then he sat in the window again. I remember he sat there without speaking for three days and three nights; all of a sudden I saw that he was crying. He was just sitting there, sir, and crying like anything; a perfect stream, as though he didn't know how his tears were flowing. And it's a sad thing, sir, to see a grown-up man and an old man, too, crying from woe and grief.

"'What's the matter, Emelyanoushka?' said I.

"He began to tremble so that he shook all over. I spoke to him for the first time since that evening.

"'Nothing, Astafy Ivanovitch.'

"'God be with you, Emelyanoushka, what's lost is lost. Why are you moping about like this?' I felt sorry for him.

"'Oh, nothing, Astafy Ivanovitch, it's no matter. I want to find some work to do, Astafy Ivanovitch.'

"'And what sort of work, pray, Emelyanoushka?'

"'Why, any sort; perhaps I could find a situation such as I used to have. I've been already to ask Fedosay Ivanitch. I don't like to be a burden on you, Astafy Ivanovitch. If I can find a situation, Astafy Ivanovitch, then I'll pay it you all back, and make you a return for all your hospitality.'

"'Enough, Emelyanoushka, enough; let bygones be bygones—and no more to be said about it. Let us go on as we used to do before.'

"'No, Astafy Ivanovitch, you, maybe, think—but I never touched your riding breeches.'

"'Well, have it your own way; God be with you, Emelyanoushka.'

"'No, Astafy Ivanovitch, I can't go on living with you, that's clear. You must excuse me, Astafy Ivanovitch.'

"'Why, God bless you, Emelyan Ilyitch, who's offending you and driving you out of the place—am I doing it?'

"'No, it's not the proper thing for me to live with you like this, Astafy Ivanovitch. I'd better be going.'

"He was so hurt, it seemed, he stuck to his point. I looked at him, and sure enough, up he got and pulled his old coat over his shoulders.

"'But where are you going, Emelyan Ilyitch? Listen to reason: what are you about? Where are you off to?'

"'No, good-bye, Astafy Ivanovitch, don't keep me now'—and he was blubbering again—'I'd better be going. You're not the same now.'

"'Not the same as what? I am the same. But you'll be lost by yourself like a poor helpless babe, Emelyan Ilyitch.'

"'No, Astafy Ivanovitch, when you go out now, you lock up your chest and it makes me cry to see it, Astafy Ivanovitch. You'd better let me go, Astafy Ivanovitch, and forgive me all the trouble I've given you while I've been living with you.'

"Well, sir, the man went away. I waited for a day; I expected he'd be back in the evening—no. Next day no sign of him, nor the third day either. I began to get frightened; I was so worried, I couldn't drink, I couldn't eat, I couldn't sleep. The fellow had quite disarmed me. On the fourth day I went out to look for him; I peeped into all the taverns, to inquire for him—but no,

Emelyanoushka was lost. 'Have you managed to keep yourself alive, Emelyanoushka?' I wondered. 'Perhaps he is lying dead under some hedge, poor drunkard, like a sodden log.' I went home more dead than alive. Next day I went out to look for him again. And I kept cursing myself that I'd been such a fool as to let the man go off by himself. On the fifth day it was a holiday—in the early morning I heard the door creak. I looked up and there was my Emelyanoushka coming in. His face was blue and his hair was covered with dirt as though he'd been sleeping in the street; he was as thin as a match. He took off his old coat, sat down on the chest and looked at me. I was delighted to see him, but I felt more upset about him than ever. For you see, sir, if I'd been overtaken in some sin, as true as I am here, sir, I'd have died like a dog before I'd have come back. But Emelyanoushka did come back. And a sad thing it was, sure enough, to see a man sunk so low. I began to look after him, to talk kindly to him, to comfort him.

"'Well, Emelyanoushka,' said I, 'I am glad you've come back. Had you been away much longer I should have gone to look for you in the taverns again today. Are you hungry?'

"'No, Astafy Ivanovitch.'

"'Come, now, aren't you really? Here, brother, is some cabbage soup left over from yesterday; there was meat in it; it is good stuff. And here is some bread and onion. Come, eat it, it'll do you no harm.'

"I made him eat it, and I saw at once that the man had not tasted food for maybe three days—he was as hungry as a wolf. So it was hunger that had driven him to me. My heart was melted looking at the poor dear. 'Let me run to the tavern,' thought I, 'I'll get something to ease his heart, and then we'll make an end of it. I've no more anger in my heart against you, Emelyanoushka!' I brought him some vodka. 'Here, Emelyan Ilyitch, let us have a drink for the holiday. Like a drink? And it will do you good.' He held out his hand, held it out greedily; he was just taking it, and then he stopped himself. But a minute after I saw him take it, and lift it to his mouth, spilling it on his sleeve. But though he got it to his lips he set it down on the table again.

"'What is it, Emelyanoushka?'

"'Nothing, Astafy Ivanovitch, I—sort of——'

"'Won't you drink it?'

"'Well, Astafy Ivanovitch, I'm not—sort of—going to drink any more, Astafy Ivanovitch.'

"'Do you mean you've given it up altogether, Emelyanoushka, or are you only not going to drink today?'

"He did not answer. A minute later I saw him rest his head on his hand.

"'What's the matter, Emelyanoushka, are you ill?'

"'Why, yes, Astafy Ivanovitch, I don't feel well.'

"I took him and laid him down on the bed. I saw that he really was ill: his head was burning hot and he was shivering with fever. I sat by him all day; towards night he was worse. I mixed him some oil and onion and kvass and bread broken up.

"'Come, eat some of this,' said I, 'and perhaps you'll be better.' He shook his head. 'No,' said he, 'I won't have any dinner today, Astafy Ivanovitch.'

"I made some tea for him, I quite flustered our old woman— he was no better. Well, thinks I, it's a bad look-out! The third morning I went for a medical gentleman. There was one I knew living close by, Kostopravov by name. I'd made his acquaintance when I was in service with the Bosomyagins; he'd attended me. The doctor come and looked at him. 'He's in a bad way,' said he, 'it was no use sending for me. But if you like I can give him a powder.' Well, I didn't give him a powder, I thought that's just the doctor's little game; and then the fifth day came.

"He lay, sir, dying before my eyes. I sat in the window with my work in my hands. The old woman was heating the stove. We were all silent. My heart was simply breaking over him, the good-for-nothing fellow; I felt as if it were a son of my own I was losing. I knew that Emelyanoushka was looking at me. I'd seen the man all the day long making up his mind to say something and not daring to.

"At last I looked up at him; I saw such misery in the poor fellow's eyes. He had kept them fixed on me, but when he saw that I was looking at him, he looked down at once.

"'Astafy Ivanovitch.'

"'What is it, Emelyanoushka?'

"'If you were to take my old coat to a second-hand dealer's, how much do you think they'd give you for it, Astafy Ivanovitch?'

"'There's no knowing how much they'd give. Maybe they would give me a rouble for it, Emelyan Ilyitch.'

"But if I had taken it they wouldn't have given a farthing for it, but would have laughed in my face for bringing such a trumpery thing. I simply said that to comfort the poor fellow, knowing the simpleton he was.

"'But I was thinking, Astafy Ivanovitch, they might give you three roubles for it; it's made of cloth, Astafy Ivanovitch. How could they only give one rouble for a cloth coat?'

"'I don't know, Emelyan Ilyitch,' said I, 'if you are thinking of taking it you should certainly ask three roubles to begin with.'

"Emelyanoushka was silent for a time, and then he addressed me again—

"'Astafy Ivanovitch.'

"'What is it, Emelyanoushka?' I asked.

"'Sell my coat when I die, and don't bury me in it. I can lie as well without it; and it's a thing of some value—it might come in useful.'

"I can't tell you how it made my heart ache to hear him. I saw that the death agony was coming on him. We were silent again for a bit. So an hour passed by. I looked at him again: he was still staring at me, and when he met my eyes he looked down again.

"'Do you want some water to drink, Emelyan Ilyitch?' I asked.

"'Give me some, God bless you, Astafy Ivanovitch.'

"I gave him a drink.

"'Thank you, Astafy Ivanovitch,' said he.

"'Is there anything else you would like, Emelyanoushka?'

"'No, Astafy Ivanovitch, there's nothing I want, but I—sort of——'

"'What?'

"'I only——'

"'What is it, Emelyanoushka?'

"'Those riding breeches——it was——sort of——I who took them——Astafy Ivanovitch.'

"'Well, God forgive you, Emelyanoushka,' said I, 'you poor, sorrowful creature. Depart in peace.'

"And I was choking myself, sir, and the tears were in my eyes. I turned aside for a moment.

"'Astafy Ivanovitch——'

"I saw Emelyanoushka wanted to tell me something; he was trying to sit up, trying to speak, and mumbling something. He flushed red all over suddenly, looked at me . . . then I saw him turn white again, whiter and whiter, and he seemed to sink away all in a minute. His head fell back, he drew one breath and gave up his soul to God."